Wreath Island
Witches Revenge

Peggy Lockwood

WREATH ISLAND/WITCHES REVENGE
Copyright © 2022 by Peggy Lockwood

All rights reserved. No part of this publication may be reproduced, distributed, or transmitted in any form or by any means, including photocopying, recording, or other electronic or mechanical methods, without the prior written permission of the publisher or author, except in the case of brief quotations embodied in critical reviews and certain other noncommercial uses permitted by copyright law.

Although every precaution has been taken to verify the accuracy of the information contained herein, the author and publisher assume no responsibility for any errors or omissions. No liability is assumed for damages that may result from the use of information contained within.

Library of Congress Control Number: 2022921855
ISBN-13: Paperback: 978-1-64749-858-0
Epub: 978-1-64749-859-7

Printed in the United States of America

GoToPublish LLC
1-888-337-1724
www.gotopublish.com
info@gotopublish.com

CONTENTS

Prologue v
Chapter 1 1
Chapter 2 3
Chapter 3 7
Chapter 4 9
Chapter 5 13
Chapter 6 17
Chapter 7 21
Chapter 8 25
Chapter 9 29
Chapter 10 33
Chapter 11 37
Chapter 12 41
Chapter 13 45
Chapter 14 47
Chapter 15 51
Chapter 16 55
Chapter 17 59
Chapter 18 63
Chapter 19 67
Chapter 20 71
Chapter 21 75
Chapter 22 77
Chapter 23 79
Chapter 24 83
Epilogue/Ashes 87

PROLOGUE

Dark clouds formed over the moon, casting eerie shadows through the trees. The air felt like the beginning of a storm. Not a regular storm when the skies open up and pour gallons of water over the countryside but more of an evil storm. For the dark wasn't just shadows, there was something else. Something you just couldn't put your finger on but knew it was there. Jane had to travel to her house on the only path through the woods. Normally, she would make sure she wasn't out this late, but the class she taught at the local school had run later than usual because of a guest speaker.

He was giving a lecture on Old Folklore in the area including these very woods. He had gone to some length about the witches and ghosts of the past. Jane had never believed in witchcraft and she certainly was not afraid of ghosts. However, this man she found had been a master in storytelling, and even as an unbeliever she felt a shiver run down her back as she made her way with only the dim light of her flashlight.

Pulling her coat close around her, she quickened her step toward home. It had just been dusk when she left the school but now the darkness of night had settled and a light rain had begun to fall. As she moved on, she was sure there had been a slight movement to the right and fear stopped her in her tracks. The trees had taken on an ominous look, and the falling rain moved the leaves back and forth as it fell. Playing her light slowly from side to side, she checked the trees on both sides of the path. There was nothing. Calling out there was only silence.

Laughing at her foolishness, she once again tightened her coat around her and started out for the small cottage the school board had supplied for her when she had first come to the island to teach. She had been happy when she saw the cottage as it was a fair distance away from the village and gave her the privacy she wanted when she wasn't at the school. She had no intention of becoming involved with the village during her private hours and the cottage in the woods gave her that freedom. However, tonight as she made her way in the dark, she thought being in the village might have its advantage, as by now she would be curled up in front of her fire in cosy slippers sipping her last cup of tea for the night.

Leaving her thoughts, she realized the dark had become black as pitch. There were no longer stars to be seen and the moon that had given some light earlier was gone. The wind too had changed, becoming more vicious and whipped around her as she tried to move on, dropping leaves from surrounding trees and holding her to the spot. Suddenly, she knew she had to get out of the woods but was unable to break loose from the spell that seemed to be holding her. Crying out helplessly, she began to sink to her knees, the black of night enveloping her.

Looking up, she saw a light just ahead coming toward her. A glimmer of hope appeared as she was sure it was someone from the village coming to help her. She would be safe again. As the light came closer, she felt the blackness loosen its grip. Then she felt a soft blanket surround her and she settled into it. It took only a moment for the warmth to take over and she was soaring high above the ground as if on a winged bird. Closing her eyes, she let the feeling close over her and suddenly the blackness became sleep.

CHAPTER 1

Sheila leaned forward against the railing of the pleasure boat winding its way through the swells toward the island. It was almost hypnotic watching the waves lap against the side of the boat spreading white foam out into the large body of water. She could hardly believe she was coming back to the island. As a small child she had thought how much fun it would be to live here. There would be no way to leave except by the vacation boat that docked every hour during the summer months and every three hours the rest of the year.

Stepping back from the railing she turned and gazed toward the island. From here everything looked pretty much the same. Just a pleasant spot to spend a summer weekend, or if you were lucky enough, an even more pleasant place to live. Suddenly, from somewhere she felt a slight stirring and the feeling of something unfolding that she had placed there long ago never to unfold again. A shiver ran down her spine and she pulled her summer sweater close around her shoulders. Taking the empty seat behind her, she closed her eyes and tried to blank out the memories that seemed to be fast returning.

A sudden jolt of the boat brought her back to reality and her thoughts folded slowly back into place. She had been so into them that she didn't realize they had arrived until the boat skimmed the edge of the dock. She waited for her fellow passengers to move ahead of her taking her time glancing toward the island itself. Yes it seemed the same. The same group of elderly men seated smoking their pipes and watching the people disembark.

As the last person walked down the narrow gangplank to the landing below she moved toward the exit and took her place in line. Now she would have to decide whether to stay on the island or make the trip back over the water once more and put the place out of her mind forever. As her foot touched the first step she paused and glanced upward toward the hill on her right. The trees were taller of course, as they had ten years growth behind them and the beach below had receded from the lake pounding against it, all was still there. To the right tall and formidable trees dominated the hill leading to her Grandfathers' house where she would be staying temporarily.

Then when she was the only one left on the boat she shook the memories further back into her mind and followed the other passengers to the upper landing. Yet as her foot touched the sandy ground she still had a slight feeling of foreboding. It was no more than a shiver but not one brought on by the cold. Sheila wanted to turn around but the captain was urging people ashore so he could return for a second group waiting on the other side of the bay.

Once again she felt something stirring in the back of her mind. It was something she knew she didn't want to remember. It went back to the time she was a child of ten. She knew that whatever had happened when she and her mother stayed here ten years ago was best forgotten but still it haunted her. Yet, the pull of the island had finally won bringing her back to teach at the school in the woods. Now she was committed and there was no turning back. Finally facing her commitment she continued across the sand to face whatever was to come.

CHAPTER 2

Emily had watched the dock for more than an hour. It had been 10 years since she had seen her friend. They had kept in touch but not nearly as often as they had intended. She remembered the first time Sheila had come to the island to stay. She was to visit her grandfather who owned the large house at the entrance to the forest. Even though she came every summer with her mother during school vacation as a small child, when her father passed away, this was the first time she would be there when school started and would attend the island school house with Emily. Emily didn't have many friends as her mother was the local charwoman and the other children shunned her, so the thought of someone new to help fill her days made her summer worth waiting for.

Now she stood once again at the top of the hill overlooking the Bay. The only thing changed was their age. Looking out over the water she could still see the dock on the other side of the Bay in spite of the new growth around her. Being here brought memories of another time. She watched as the sun filtered little streaks of colour through the trees and settled on the rippling water just beneath her. It was a magic place full of fairy stories with unicorns and other things of childhood. She remembered standing right here with Sheila standing on tip toe, both of them reaching for the fairies flying overhead.

Suddenly the ferry horn blew and startled her back to reality. She glanced down the hill toward the dock where the boat was just pulling in. Scanning the deck she searched for her friend wondering if she would know her after all this time. Then just above the heads of the crowd she saw a hand waving in her direction and realized Sheila remembered their secret spot too and could see her now. Picking up her skirts and waving her arms in delight she took off down the hill to meet her friend. They nearly collided as they crossed the sand. Sheila dropped her bag and ran the last steps into Emily's arms. The ten years since they had seen each other suddenly disappeared making it seem like yesterday. As children they had pledged their friendship for life. Now looking at Emily she knew they had been wrong not staying in touch. For a moment they just stood looking at each other and then arms linked started up the hill chattering like children.

Sheila felt a sudden rush of being home. It was as if she had been here all along. Both girls were oblivious to the crowd making their way to the local restaurant visible from the boat dock. Emily had written her letting her know that their friend Tom had purchased the business the year before and they planned on stopping there first. She wondered if she would know him after all this time. They had been a foursome every summer during her childhood. The three of them and Andy, who also stayed on the island and joined the police force. They had been so close as children yet now she knew so little of them. In fact she remembered very little of any of her time here. It was as if a blanket had been spread over her memory and was too heavy to lift.

She shook herself back to the present and realized Emily had been chattering on since they started up the hill. Now they had come to the top standing in front of Tom's restaurant and were about to enter. She hoped she hadn't missed too much during her time away. The sound of the boat whistle brought her back to reality and glancing back down the hill she watched the boat glide softly into the bay. Taking Emily's hand she turned toward the restaurant hoping she could pick up the conversation where she left off and restart her life over again.

CHAPTER 3

Sheila rolled over and faced the window in the large upstairs bedroom. For a moment she couldn't remember where she was. She watched as the sunbeams raced across the ceiling and settled on the dressing table on the far wall. It was a pretty room, one she had spent many days in as a child. Some of them pleasant and others she chose not to remember. Childhood had not been happy for her. Some of the less pleasant times she had spent in her grandfather's house.

At first everything had seemed like fun until she learned that evil had two faces. One that is used to deceive the young and the innocent and the other that shows its' true face once you are defeated. Such innocence in children she thought had been betrayed that summer. How easy it was to make them see what you wanted them to see and not what was really there. She and Emily had nearly crossed the line of no return that summer of long ago in their search for someone to care. If it hadn't been for each other they might not be here today to tell the tale.

Glancing up at the ceiling she watched as the sunbeams that a moment ago were bright and cheerful slowly became dark shadows that were not inviting at all. Pulling the covers tightly around her chin she slipped further down into the bed away from the reality of the day. For a few moments she lay very still with hope that when she opened her eyes again she would find herself back in her warm bed in her New York apartment. The first feeling of course would just be one more of her nightmares that she could not shake off.

She lay quiet for one moment longer and then slowly opened her eyes to the room around her. Pushing the covers away from her face she was now able to see that it was indeed not her apartment but the reality of the nightmare she had been having since she was a child in her grandfathers' house. The sun was shining through a slit at the bottom of the window shade and little dots raced across the blankets at the foot of her bed. Well, at least it was not a dreary day. It would make it much easier to spend the time she had to in her grandfather's house before she went on to the cottage that was to be hers during her stay on the island. She needed Emily and the security and courage she would bring.

Throwing back the covers she slipped over the side of the bed and into her slippers. She crossed the room and raised the blind glancing into the yard surrounding the house. It was a large yard stretching to the cliff on one side then circling to the right toward the hill leading down to the bay. She couldn't see far to the left because of the out buildings but she knew that just behind the stables was a narrow path leading to a dense forest of pine trees that held any sunlight from entering.

It was at the other end of this forest that the school house stood where she would be teacher for the next year. It was also where another small path led to the cottage that she would call home while she was there. She could have stayed with her grandfather but the thought of travelling through the forest each day to reach the school had decided her to take the offer of the cottage supplied by the school board. By daylight she could see the roof of the cottage from the schoolyard and she didn't intend to be at the school house after dark, ever. Now, fully dressed she was ready to face the day and her grandfather. Slipping into her jacket she made her way down the stairs and a start to a new life.

CHAPTER 4

The old man had tossed restlessly on his bed. He stood with his hands in his pockets gazing over the back towards the barn. This had been a happy spot and a happy stance for him over the years. He remembered when he was young and newly married standing right here looking towards his future. Now he had not been able to sleep for the two nights that the girl had been in the house. It had been necessary to say yes to her staying here as the cottage was not ready for her to move in. She was after all his granddaughter. He had watched as she disembarked from the boat and felt once again a moment of fear. The same fear he had experienced when she had arrived with her mother as a small child. They had stayed for a year and in that time all the old fears had come back to haunt him. It had surprised him that she wanted to return. Her mother was gone now so there was no one to dissuade her from her decision to become a teacher.

The school had been run by a part time teaching staff for the past ten years in the basement of the local church as no one had wanted to teach in the school house. He wanted this to be a permanent arrangement. However, the island School Board such as it was wanted something better and had placed an ad in the mainland paper for a permanent position. Now he feared the island secrets would be revealed. He thought about the last time he had this feeling. It had been Halloween, 10 years ago.

He had suggested a guest speaker for the night of All Hallows Eve. It was the final week of festivities and would wind up the summer for the island. He had also been fortunate enough to find a professor well known for researching Historical events. It had been his luck that the man was free on this particular weekend and had agreed to come. They would use the school house a short distance from his house for the lecture well out of the way of the village.

The night arrived dark and eerie and many who attended were nervous about returning to their homes at the end of the evening, the local teacher being one of them. She lived in the small cottage within sight of the school house but it was still very dark and isolated from the village. The cottage had been one of the focal points of the professors' talk. The evening right from the beginning had been a huge success and the committee along with himself patted themselves on the back and headed for their homes at the end beaming with satisfaction.

The next morning however, they found that the school teacher was missing. Where had she gone? Was the history of the island so disturbing that she had somehow found a way back to the mainland and disappeared totally from view. A search had been made of the island but she was never found and the only boat was still where it had been the night before. The school had been closed and the children moved into the village church where their studies were continued. Now it would open again and his granddaughter would be teaching there. The old man couldn't help but fear this would open the door once more to the secrets of Wreath Island.

He thought at the time the teacher disappeared there had not been a thorough enough search as all her possessions were still at the cottage. Nothing had been moved. It had been searched well that first night and the next morning the school board members had re-entered for a more thorough search.

However, there were no clues as to the teachers' whereabouts and after a short period of time and checking her former address they went on to other things. The building had been closed and the children moved to another place of learning. There had been nothing that happened to change where the school was held and no one seemed to notice the difference.

All had been quiet until now when the school board decided to re-open the school to a new teacher. Then his granddaughter having seen the ad for a teacher applied for the position. He had never dreamed that this would happen and he would be thrown back into the past. None of this had suited him but he was one person voting against a full committee and he lost. For many years he had shied away from Halloween, never letting the village know how involved he really was in the night. In his mind he went back to his life as a young man when the village elders had come to him offering a position that now he wished he had never accepted.

It was the time of the witch trials. They were being practiced over the entire country but none more than on his own door step of Wreath Island. He was both frightened and pleased at the offer however now wished he had listened to his own voice and refused what the committee considered an honour. It wasn't easy to recognise witches as they were very careful to keep their identity hidden from their friends and neighbours. Due to this he would never be known to anyone except the small committee of his involvement. He alone would be in charge of finding and ridding the island of any witches living among the residents. He felt very important at first rounding up and branding witch on anyone who crossed him or even looking like they would cross them. It was to be a secret from the village and even his family just in case one of them might hold the position of witch. He was given a silver locket with a picture taken with him and the next branded witch.

He had branded many friends over the years but now the picture was that of his granddaughter and he had no recourse but to finish the job. There was no way out for him and he knew he would have to mark her for the dreaded death bestowed on the so named witches. Now they were ready to start again what he feared would be the old ways. He tried to shake this from his mind and decided the best thing to do would be to go and see his granddaughter. She should after all if for the sake of the village people look like she was welcome in his home. With a sigh he threw back the covers and slipped off the side of the bed. It would be, he knew a very long day.

CHAPTER 5

Sheila took the large brass key from her pocket and slowly inserted it into the door of the old school house. It was a heavy wooden door and did not move easily beneath her hand. She had to put her shoulder against it to move it at all and even this did not happen on the first push. It felt like the door was pushing back against her not wanting her to enter. Finally with loud objection it moved under her weight and she fell into the room. All the windows were still sealed from the winter so the room had a dark hazy look about it.

Sheila felt a shiver run up her back as the cold musty air settled over her. Once again somewhere in her mind stirred something from the past that was unpleasant. She stood still for just a moment feeling the dark settle around her. It was as if there was something or someone in the room with her. She could hear her own breathing and the sound of her heart beating.

She wanted to turn and run as fast as she could to the boat landing and a way back home. Home, she thought with a smile, somewhere she had given up to come back to the island. It should have been over, yet something still seemed to be driving her back to a place where she had very few fond memories and yet some others as well. Suddenly Sheila was brought out of her reverie by something soft and furry brushing against her arm. Not able to move she held her breath as the feeling moved up against her neck and across her back. Then she heard it, a tiny little laugh as if coming from a very small child. No more than a tinkle but certainly a laugh. It was gone as quick as it came, as was the soft fur and once again she was alone.

She shook herself and moved to the nearest window and released the shutters. Sunshine filled the room revealing only the small desks and black board across the one wall. She made her way around the room releasing the remainder of the shutters looking for whatever had touched her. Now that was better she thought as sunlight fell across the room giving everything a golden glow. Sheila remembered this room although she had only attended school here for one year. She and her mother had come to stay with her grandfather again after her father died, yet the place seemed like home to her more than her own.

To begin with it had seemed like an adventure for a 10 year old. The island had always been a fun place for her when they came to visit and the idea of living here for a whole year had been exciting. She would have all that time with her friend Emily who lived on the island. Sheila had always thought her friend so lucky never having to leave. However, as the year progressed things changed and Sheila found that the island had another side. Not one she wanted to pursue at this time or any other for that matter.

With a shake Sheila pushed away these thoughts and turned to the front of the class and the large desk that was to be hers. Her mother had wanted her to train for a different profession but the further she went in school the more she realized that teaching was where she belonged. So when her mother had passed away a few months before she graduated she made her own choice to teach. Her final spell of luck happened when the position for a teacher came up at the school on the island. It was as though it had just been waiting for her to finish school to join them.

Now here she was standing once more in the school of her childhood waiting for something to complete her life.

Reaching down she ran her fingers over the smooth surface of the large old desk. She felt a slight tingle as her fingertips met the scars of the pen nibs of the past. The tingle ran up her arm until it reached the nape of her neck and she once again felt dread and maybe some fear at being here. Once again the tiny laugh came from around her and the soft touch of something laid on her arm. It lingered for just a moment then was gone.

She felt a sudden darkness drop around her until it enveloped everything in the room. Then from the corner of her eye she caught what seemed to be a flash of light followed once more by the sound of a child's laughter. Fear mounted in her chest and she was frozen to the spot. It took a moment for her heart to slow to a normal beat. She slowly opened her eyes and glanced around. A sudden knocking on the door brought her back to reality and the darkness that had come over her faded. It took a moment or two to realize where she was. Once more she glanced around the room and thought how well everything had been set up for her. It was as if all had been decided 10 years before on Halloween and the island was just waiting for her to grow up and fit into the mould. She found this a bit scary and wondered if things like this were actually possible. Annoyed she made her way across the room forming words in her mind that she would greet the unwelcomed visitor with. She brushed the dust from her skirt and stopped for a moment at the wall mirror to check her hair. Glancing at her watch she realized it could be Emily. She put on a smile of greeting and moved to open the door unaware of the sound of wings moving slowly overhead with each move she made.

CHAPTER 6

Emily pulled the window curtains back and looked out over the Bay. It seemed quiet this morning. This surprised her for usually the day after the boat arrived from the mainland the small village was bustling with what the island called those summer people. Today however, only the locals wandered the streets. She was a little disappointed as she was sure her own excitement must have spilled over somewhat at the arrival of her friend.

She glanced toward the end of the street where the hill began that wound its way up towards the school house where she was to meet Sheila. She opened her small window and took a breath of the first air of the morning. Yes, it would be another perfect fall day. Just right for her friends return. She turned and surveyed the space that she called home. Since the death of her mother she had rented a small space in the local inn. Now she was aware at how small her domain was. There was only room for her bed, one dresser and a rocker and table by the window. Also, there was a small area set up as a bathroom where she had the luxury of her own shower stall.

Recently she had purchased a small bookshelf that stood against the wall just inside the door that she was busy filling each week with her beloved books. It didn't look much different than the other rooms in the inn except for the bright blue cover on the bed and the matching curtains on the window.

These she had purchased with her first pay check from the local coffee shop where she had worked since leaving school. The material had been on sale at the notions shop next door to the coffee shop and she had loved its' happy appearance.

Life had been pretty uneventful for her except for Andy of course. When they were children she and Andy along with Sheila and Tom had been constant companions and the year that Sheila had lived on the island they had spent many wonderful days together. They also had many adventures. She was suddenly aware of a haze across her eyes and when she tried to think of some of their adventures she found she was unable to bring them back. A knock on the door brought her back to reality and she realized she had been standing day dreaming when she should have been getting ready for work.

Taking a final look in the long mirror on her door to see if she was indeed all together she opened the door to Andy standing in the hall. From the time she had started working Andy had arrived each morning to walk her to work. This morning was a short shift as she had promised Tom she would work the first two hours of her day off just to look after the early morning breakfast crowd. Then she was off to the school house to help Sheila clean things up for the first day of school in the old building.

Linking arms with Andy she set off down the hall. She glanced at him as they made their way down the old staircase. He didn't look any different than he had when they were in school together. They had always been considered a pair and most of their friends kept waiting for the magic day of marriage to happen. Since both had come from a rather poor background they had decided that they would make sure they had a small nest egg before they took this step. However, Andy had recently been promoted to Deputy Sheriff so the big day seemed much closer than ever before.

They continued hand in hand to the coffee shop where Emily said goodbye and went in to put in her time for the day. The time would go fast as she was not working a full shift. Finally with her time over she dropped her apron over a nail behind the kitchen door and waving goodbye to Tom she headed out the door and toward Sheila and the school house.

Emily was almost running as she reached the top of the hill. She knew Sheila's grandfather would probably be watching her from the upstairs window of the grand house he owned at the edge of the forest. She had always been afraid of this house as a child and fear did not abate as she grew older.

Her mother had not allowed her to come to the forest until Sheila came to the island to live, then she and Sheila along with Andy and Tom came there almost daily looking for adventures. When Sheila left once again the mountain left her life. She missed the stories they wove about fairies and Unicorns and if she were asked today she would tell people that some of it was true.

As she entered the forest she slowed her pace and stepped cautiously onto the school path. It was so dark that looking down she was unable to see her feet. The slight breeze caused a movement ahead of her and she could feel the difference in the coolness of the air. Also, she was sure she saw a movement in the bushes to her right. Slowing her steps even more she looked from side to side for a possible small animal or a flutter of breeze, but there was none.

Suddenly frightened she wanted to retrace her steps and head for the safeness of her home and the lock of her door. Then remembering Sheila was waiting for her she turned and raced toward the school. Suddenly there it was her old school house just as she remembered it. Turning, she looked back over the path into the dark and then with one final run reached the small stoop that served as a porch and falling up the steps she pounded heavily on the door.

CHAPTER 7

The old man stood in the upstairs window of the old house overlooking the village below. He spent most of his days here just watching and sorting the villagers into categories for later use. It had been a long time since he was able to look out the window without fear. As a young man he had been offered the position of sorting the villagers into groups for future reference. At the time it seemed both exciting and important. It wasn't until later that he found this was a position he would no longer keep for a short time but it was a position he would hold for life. He fingered the silver locket he held in his hand feeling it move until the chain was wound tightly around his fingers making him unable to move from the spot. Telling him how permanent his position was.

Moving over to the fireplace he lifted the small silver box buried behind the large brass candle sticks. It had been buried there for the past 10 years, gathering dust, where he had hoped never to touch it again. He had placed it there himself after that fatal night 10 years ago. That was the night the professor had come to lecture at the school about the history of Wreath Island. Tonight the people would learn about Terror Trail. Something that had been kept secret for many years. It was also the night the small silver box would be presented to the world. For many years it had been hidden away with only the old man knowing about it and the secret it held. The clasp had been sealed to hide the picture inside and the meaning behind it.

It had just been a bit of Halloween fun at the time having someone bring the history of the island to life. The whole evening had been arranged by the village council to bring more people over from the mainland and also a way to make some extra money for repairs on the building the council and police department called home. It had needed repair for some time but with limited families living permanently on the island there had not been enough in taxes to look after them. So the council had decided that celebrating All Hallows Eve with a candle walk and terror trail along with games for the children and food of course from the local ladies might just be the way to pick up the extra money they needed. The professor had been his idea as a way to start the ball rolling then followed by the rest of the program ending up in the forest with a candle walk. The council agreed and so the first All Hallows Eve celebration for the island was set in stone. He had regretted this decision every day since.

He looked down at the silver box in his hand. He could almost feel it move. Such a small container to hold such a large secret. He had tried to shut that night out of his mind and had nearly succeeded until he heard his granddaughter would be coming back to teach at the local school house in the forest. Now it was all returning. The disappearance of the school teacher at the time of the Halloween Eve celebration was something that to this day had never been explained. Nor had the night of monsters and darkness and a fear that had engulfed the whole island. Now it was starting over and he was afraid once more.

Still holding the box he dropped to his knees in front of the burning fire. He had never known such fear. He knew that if he made this move it might prove fatal to him and possibly his granddaughter as well. If only he could go back through the years and erase the part of the past that held him. He knew that it had to be finished now. For only a moment he hesitated, then lifting the box over his head he hurled it into the flame. The room turned suddenly dark. No light came from the window or from the blaze of the fire before him. The old man crouched in fear gazing into what had just a moment ago been just a blazing beautiful fire.

He watched as the silver box lifted from the embers and began to glow. He was unable to move away and knelt in fear as the box moved toward him. It swirled slowly above his head for a moment then the lid slowly began to open. Unable to move he watched as a dark cloud rose from inside the box. He never felt fear as dark as this and knew he never would again. He remembered his granddaughter and realized by allowing the box to open he had put her life in peril.

He lifted his arm to push the box away but it was too late. A dark cloud rose from inside the box and slowly one by one eight black crows rose from the box landing on him engulfing everything in darkness in a blanket of black. He watched as each one settled on his arms and shoulders engulfing him till the light was gone. He could feel the darkness folding around him as he sank to the floor. He had gone too far. There was no return for him. Memories of the past washed over him. Bad memories that could not be erased. He wished he could take his past and relive it as the person he should have been. He knew this could not happen and he was condemned to a life he had signed up for years before. Just before he gave into the darkness he was able to see what it was that would destroy his granddaughter and the island with it. As the final curtain fell he heard a voice say, "Not this time old man." Then he slipped away into a river of darkness.

CHAPTER 8

The local coffee shop was a beehive of activity this morning. It seemed like everyone from the village and some had come out for an early breakfast. This time of year was always busy. However, this weekend would top off everything for the whole year. Tom stood behind the cash register looking over the noisy crowd, wondering if he had put in enough supplies to look after the crowd for three days. He slipped into the kitchen to check with his staff. The village expected a large crowd from the mainland as they had advertised a long list of activities. Every town in the Boston, Plymouth area celebrated All Hallows Eve. However, this year Wreath Island held the most for tourists before the ferry stopped running its summer schedule.

After making sure all was well in the kitchen he poured himself another cup of coffee and made his way to the table set aside for the staff. Now it was time to check over the events the committee had scheduled. Tom had been on the committee since he opened the coffee shop two years ago thinking it would keep him in the middle of things. Also, it was good for business to be seen active in the village and he intended to spend his life here.

He reached into the cabinet behind him and pulled out a folder marked committee notes, then settled down to go over the details for the night before the second string of customers arrived for lunch. Running his fingers down the first page he felt a slight tremor. Pulling his arm away he looked at the sheet of paper before him. There didn't seem to be anything about it that might cause a shock, yet it felt almost like glass shards. Cautiously he touched a corner of the paper again. This time nothing. Smiling to himself he glanced around to see if anyone had been aware of his strange reaction.

To his surprise he found no one in the shop moving. The conversation around him had stopped and the room seemed as if frozen in time. For a moment he sat very still and closing his eyes tried to get some control on what was happening. After a moment of sitting still he slowly opened his eyes to an empty room that just a moment before had been a bustling coffee shop filled with noisy happy people. He also was unable to move and watched as the paper moved slowly under his hand. Now he could feel panic rising and he was aware of a whispering in his ears and the air becoming almost frigid around him.

He watched helplessly as his fingers began to move over the paper tracing the words that were echoing in his mind. He traced each one in turn and realized he could see the words not by sight but in his mind. He traced each letter to the bottom of the page. As he touched the last word the air turned warm and he could hear the sound of people laughing around him. Looking around he checked to see if anyone else had been aware of what was happening but found all intent on their own conversation with no awareness of his movement. For a moment he sat very still then reached for his coffee. He found his hands shaking and in spite of the recent cold in the air it was as hot as if he had just poured it. He glanced at the paper before him. Grasping the edge of the table he lowered his eyes. There in capital letters were the words.

      ONCE MORE HALLOWEEN, REMEMBER?
            ARE YOU PREPARED?

He watched as his knuckles turned white and a memory of long forgotten formed in his mind. Tom stared straight ahead into the past as the dark began to settle around him. He felt himself falling. Just as he was sinking he was aware of a hand on his shoulder. Looking up he found Andy grinning down at him. Through a fog he watched as Andy settled in the chair opposite and poured himself a cup of coffee unaware of a problem. Closing the book and trying to steady his hand from shaking he tried to look as normal as possible for his visit with Andy.

CHAPTER 9

Professor Jacobs pushed his chair back from the desk. He glanced down at the open letter in front of him. It was from an old acquaintance from his school days. Included was a clipping from Wreath Island News announcing the All Hallows Eve weekend. His friend was asking him to speak on the history of the island as part of the festivities that weekend. This was the one drawback to his position as history professor. Everyone thought he spent his time researching the entire country.

However, Wreath Island was close at hand. He had spent his life on the mainland spending most summers on the island with and aunt and uncle. Even as a youngster he had pried into everything he could find out about the island earning himself the name of that pesky little kid. The most interesting had been in the 1800's at the time of the witch hunts when from Boston to Cape Cod and all the other local villages along the sea coast drowned and burned witches daily. He reached for his pipe and tobacco pouch and crossed to the window. Silently he gazed out across the Bay.

One story came to mind that had always intrigued him. There had been two local lads who had married two local sisters. After their marriages they had pretty much kept to themselves running a small farm on the island keeping sheep and cattle. They did not attend the local church much to the distress of the Parson and many other inhabitants on the island. The women were not involved with the community as most of the other women were. Some of the women had spoken to the parson about this and raised his suspicion enough to have him visit the family.

It had been mid-afternoon the day he chose to visit the ladies when both men were out working in their fields. When the Parson arrived everything was quiet at the farm house. Stepping up on the front porch he leaned over to peek in the front window. At first he saw nothing and assumed there was no one home. He was just about to turn away when he noticed a small flicker of light in the corner of a far room.

It was coming from what he supposed to be one of the bedrooms. Leaning further over the porch rail he was just able to see the women of the house kneeling before a small table filled with candles. One of the sisters seemed to be pouring a small amount of liquid from a large metal pitcher into glass jars. He watched fascinated as her sister dropped wicks into the jars and set them aside. Meanwhile her sister kept a flame hot under a pot of black liquid which she poured into the jars keeping enough of the wick over the top of the jar to steady it. After the liquid was added they set the pots aside once more to set. Why, he thought they were making candles.

Suddenly it occurred to him they were not just candles. They were black candles, witches candles. He froze for a moment not able to move because of what he had seen. Then he realized with a shock these women were witches. Quietly he pushed back from the window and hurried silently down the steps rushing toward the village eager to let the local police know what he had seen. He found himself shaking with what he had learned. Right here on their own little island they were living with witches.

Hurrying to his church he let himself in and for the first time he could remember poured himself a large glass of communion wine. After a few minutes his hands were steady once more and he was able to think about what he had to do next. He could just ignore what he had seen and tell the ladies of the village he had been too busy to visit the farm. How easy that would be.

He tried to justify the candles and could have if they had been any other colour but black. Everyone knew that black candles were symbolic of witchcraft and stayed away from them for their own safety. He reached for his pipe and was glad to see he finally had a good steady hand. The other option of course was to think of the village people and their safety. Lighting his pipe he settled down in his favourite chair to think things over. Finally when he was sure he had control of his feelings he set his pipe aside and headed into the village and the sheriff.

They would have to settle this now, before the witches got control. They were still new enough to the village to find a reason to move them out. He quickened his step making his way across the village to the sheriff's office. Opening the door he found no one there. How strange the door was unlocked and the building empty. He made his way to the front counter and tapped impatiently to attract the attention of anyone in the back room. There was no time to waste. The moment the witches had control the village would belong to them and no one would ever be safe again. Once more he raised his hand and pounded on the counter. This time with more gusto.

He knew he had to stop this even before it started. So many people were in danger. As a man of the cloth it was his duty to save them now. There was still no answer from the back. He was about to bang again when a door to the back room opened and the sheriff entered the room. He breathed a sigh of relief as finally he knew the village would be safe.

CHAPTER 10

The local sheriff was just about to close up for the day. It was a bit early as nothing had happened to even write a report about since he opened the office this morning. At times he wished for the busy office back in Boston where he had spent the best half of his life. Now there was a city that understood law enforcement. Law and order was just that, law and order. He wondered what possessed him to put in for a transfer to such a lonely place.

It seemed like such a wonderful opportunity at the time. He could see long summer evenings sitting on the dock with a fishing rod in his hand. Maybe long coffee breaks at the local diner chewing the fat with the old boys. It didn't take long for him to find out that the local old boys weren't interested in spending time with anyone wearing a badge. Because of this he had found it a lonely life on the island. If something didn't happen soon he would be putting in for a transfer for back home.

He was just checking the door and windows in the back when he heard someone enter the front office. Pulling his coat from the coat rack he headed toward the front office to tell whoever it was they would have to wait until morning when the office opened again. After all how important could it be in a place this small. Turning off the overhead light he opened the door to the main office.

Parson White stood patiently at the small front desk. It seemed strange coming here at this time of night. During the day there was the hustle and bustle of people moving around and the chatter of the office girl going about her normal days' work. Now everything was quiet and most of the lights had been turned off for the night. He could hear someone moving around in the back and assumed it was the sheriff getting ready to go home.

He stood patiently at the counter waiting until he saw the door to the holding rooms open. Then bracing himself against the counter for support he proceeded to tell the sheriff what he had seen. The sheriff's face turned white as he listened to the story from the local parson. His knuckles also turned white as he gripped the edge of the desk and a red look of anger crossed his face. It didn't take long for the sheriff to make a decision. Pulling on his coat he ushered the Parson out onto the street. He knew a group of men in the village he could count on in such a disaster. Women too for that matter. He would have to hurry to catch these families in their folly.

Within the hour the men and some women had grouped in the centre of town and with weapons held high headed out to the small farm at the edge of the village. It was a beautiful quiet night at the farm when they arrived. The two women had finished their candle making and prepared supper for their husbands. They were pleased at how many candles they had been able to put together with a hope that the villagers would buy them the following week at the All Hallows Eve celebration. Both women were very shy, even more now the one was pregnant. Their husbands had told them they had to make friends with other ladies so all the family would be accepted as part of the village.

After much thought they decided they would make candles to sell the following week on All Hallows Eve. After all everyone needed candles and it was something they were quite good at. Now decision made, 100 beautiful black candles were ready and stored in boxes waiting to be transported to the festival. With supper over and the kitchen tidy the women decided to join their husbands who were contentedly smoking their pipes on the front porch enjoying the evening breeze. They were hardly out the front door when they noticed a large group of men and women headed their way. Both of their husbands noticed them too and stood to welcome the group, hands outstretched in friendship. It was only at the last moment the men saw the group was armed and not at all friendly. There was no time to ask why this was happening or to try to get away. Their cries could not be heard for the shouts of the people.

Before they could protect themselves the group of men pulled both couples from the porch and dragged them across the lawn to a large oak tree at the edge of the Bay. Here they hanged all four side by side and left them there. There was total silence as the bodies swung from their ropes. Finally all was quiet with no sound at all in the warm summer evening. Then one by one the crowd made their way back to their homes to think over what they had done. No one would cut the bodies down or bury them so they were left hanging for the elements to take care of. This was a story unknown to today's locals as they had buried it over the years hoping it would never be told. This was the secret grandfather had been hiding for years.

Sighing, Professor Jacobs turned from the window and returned to his desk. He tapped the ashes from his pipe into the ashtray and slipped it back into the pocket of his jacket. With a slight smile he picked the letter up and read it once more. Maybe it was time for the island locals to know their history and who better to tell them than him. Smiling to himself he took a piece of paper from the desk drawer and began a letter accepting the challenge he wasn't sure he really wanted. This would start the beginning of a not wanted future he thought. He hesitated for just a moment, then pen to paper he began what would be the start of a dark dismal future.

CHAPTER 11

Sheila dusted off the last book and placing it back on the shelf glanced around the room. Yes, she thought everything was ready for the next school term. She was glad Emily had come to help her. She had thought her friend looked a bit pale when she arrived but Emily assured her she was quite alright and started right in helping with the cleanup. It had been like old times chattering away like children as they worked together.

The cleanup hadn't been as bad as she thought it might be as someone in the village had been there before them and looked after most of the heavy work. The school had been closed for 10 years and should have by rights been unfit for use. She stopped for a moment to look around her. It was in wonderful shape she thought. Where the walls should have been in poor repair they surprisingly gave the impression of freshly painted new wood. Someone had been looking after it all this time.

Now, not for the first time it crossed her mind that the school had been waiting for her to come. Not a good thought. She was suddenly aware of being alone. Realizing Emily was working the cloakroom at the front door she called out it was time for them to leave. There had been enough dust for one day and she wanted to catch up on all the local news that happened since she left. Emily came out from behind the partition defining the cloakroom and joined her. Taking a final look around to see if they had missed anything Sheila turned out the lights and locked up the school house for the night.

They were surprised to find a fine rain had started while they worked. Still chattering when they closed the door they continued up the walk until they reached the path leading to Sheila's cottage. Making arrangements to meet the next day they went their opposite ways waving until they were out of sight. Pulling her coat around her, Sheila left the main path and started toward the cottage. She was beginning to wish she had left the school sooner as it was almost dusk and there was very little light filtering between the trees. She worried about her friend walking the rest of the way alone through the woods. She remembered this feeling from a former time in her life and felt a cold shiver up her spine. She laughed suddenly as she realized she was feeling the fear of a 10 year old child. This from someone who was being given a group of young minds to mould. If the parents had any idea how nervous she was in the woods her career as a teacher would be over before it began.

She quickened her step and soon was able to see the roof of the cottage ahead. She broke through the trees into a small clearing and saw what would be her home for at least the next year. It was a pleasant little cottage, much more cheerful than the woods around it. Sheila wondered why it had been built so far away from the school when it had been intended for whoever would teach there.

Stepping onto the small porch she turned to look back into the woods. She was surprised to find the schoolhouse was visible from her porch. Coming through the woods it had seemed further away. The porch was small but did have enough room for a tiny rocking chair and a planter full of red and blue flowers. Sheila wasn't much of a gardener but she knew enough to know that the flowers had been recently tended most likely for her arrival. She wondered if the inside had been prepared for her as well. Checking her pockets for the set of keys that included both cottage and school house she chose the one for the cottage and slipped the key into the lock. This door too was hard to open leaving Sheila with the notion that the house itself might need a good cleaning as well. However, it wasn't going to get it tonight, it could wait until tomorrow when Emily would be there. She just wanted to sleep.

She found leaning into the door finally opened it for her. However, her spirits dropped as once more the blinds were pulled giving the interior a grey dusky look. She ran her hand down the wall just inside the door hoping to find a light switch but found none. Stepping into the interior she closed the door behind her. To the left of the door she opened the window blind letting some light in. She was now able to see the rest of the room.

The rain had stopped and the last of the days' sunlight pushed its way in. As in the school she made her way from window to window until all the blinds were open. Now at the last window she turned to survey the room. To her surprise the room now flooded with light showed a very well kept living area. The front part of the room held a small couch and easy chair. In the corner stood a large writing desk flanked by ceiling to floor book shelves.

The back section held a sink, stove and icebox with a small wooden table and two chairs. There were two doors in the area as well. These she thought must be the bedroom and bathroom. She was about to explore these areas when a sudden burst of sunlight stopped her in her tracks. She had been so busy checking the space that she didn't realize how clean everything was. Stopping, she ran her finger over the book shelves the one place that might be neglected by the dust cloth. It came up clean. She was sure that had she been wearing white gloves no grime would be found.

What a wonderful surprise, she must make a note to find the cleaner and thank them. For tonight however she was looking forward to crawling into what she was sure was a fresh clean bed. Dropping her shoes beside the couch she headed for the bedroom and sleep.

CHAPTER 12

When Sheila stepped out onto the porch of her little cottage the next morning the sun was already breaking through the trees and felt warm on her arms. It was late in the season for this weather but the island always seemed to be the last place that winter set in. It was as if some power held things in abate until after Halloween made its' appearance. For the past 10 years she had bypassed this holiday, closing her doors and turning off the lights pretending it was just another day. Bur now back on the island she had to face it once more. With the celebrations officially set she would have to face the reality of All Hallows Eve as it had been 10 years ago. Most of this time had faded from her memory, partly because of her age at the time and partly because she had deliberately erased it.

She remembered how Emily, Andy, Tom and herself had planned this night the whole summer that year for what was always the best weekend of the year. Now she only thought of it with dread and bad memories. Memories she just couldn't bring to mind. Setting her thoughts aside she once more did a complete circle around the cottage outside checking the condition of windows and doors. She found this to be unnecessary as with the school the outside of the house had been seen to before her arrival. Now if she received the same treatment from the students her decision to come back was the right one. Still there was that little bit of something nagging at her that wouldn't give her peace.

Deciding it was too nice a day for bad thoughts she picked her bag up off the steps where she had left it and started down the mountain to check on her friend. As she left the small yard around the cottage she lost the sunlight and quickened her step up the path. As she reached the school house the sun broke through the trees once again and she felt her heart beat slowly at the familiar sight of the little building ahead of her. She had loved this school as a child and was sure she would love it again. Stopping for a moment she remembered the time with Emily, Tom and Andy and how they had made her time with her grandfather more bearable during her stay.

Looking ahead the forest loomed dark and sinister and she was tempted to unlock the school house and spend the day preparing lessons for the opening day. She tried peering into the forest to detect anything that might persuade her to do so but there was nothing visible. Only the thickness of the trees and underbrush. Sheila could almost draw a line where the sunlit yard ended and the darkness began. She stood in the sun for just a moment then moved behind the school and slipped into darkness.

Tom had been standing at the top of the hill looking down over the bay. It was quiet this morning belying the fact that every rental was full. It helped that the island social committee had decided to celebrate All Hallows Eve. Tapping his pipe against the tree he proceeded to fill it once more for a few final puffs before he headed down the mountain to prepare for a breakfast onslaught at the shop. As he lit a match to light his pipe a sudden breeze came up blowing it out just as he touched the side of his pipe.

That was strange there had been no breeze all the time he had been standing there. Once more he lit a match and once more a breeze came up to blow it out. He stood still for a moment testing the air with the usual practice of wet finger in the air feeling nothing. Deciding it was going to be impossible to have a smoke he dropped his pipe in his shirt pocket and was about to follow it with his matches when he decided that just once more he would try to light a match. It took several tries but finally it caught. Almost immediately a breeze came from the woods behind him blowing out the match. He could feel cold chills making their way up his back. Was this an omen of some kind? He was aware of a stillness that had not been there when he arrived. It was as if he were going back in his memory for a childhood he wanted to forget.

It seemed more than just a quiet morning in the village as he first thought. It was total stillness. There were no birds singing, no rustle of leaves in the trees, nothing. Looking up the clouds seemed to be standing still. Turning towards the woods he noticed movement just past the first line of trees. Someone was there. He watched as the figure made its way towards him. As they broke free of the woods it was as if movement had begun again and he could hear birds and rustling in the underbrush. Then he saw Sheila. He laughed when he realized how foolish he must have looked to her. Slipping the matches into his pocket he made his way across the path to meet her. It looked like it was going to be a great morning after all.

CHAPTER 13

Mary and Abigail had worked all day preparing for All Hallows Eve. It was to be their first outing since moving to Wreath Island. Many people would be coming from the mainland and the sisters hoped to be able to sell enough of their homemade candles to help with the cost of Abigail's baby. The baby would be born before the Christmas season and they wanted this to be a happy occasion.

John and William were working in the back fields today so they would be late for supper giving the sisters more time to work at their craft. It had been hard to decide what colour to use on the candles but in the end they had decided on black as it would hold the colour longer than the pale ones and also would take less colour to make. It had been a happy morning as Abigail was finally over the difficult part of her pregnancy. Her mornings had been hard and Mary was glad they were living together so she could take care of her. Now it seemed to be over and they could spend the last months getting ready for the birth.

They were putting their final touches on a group of candles when Mary thought she heard a noise on the front porch. She hesitated for only a moment then made her way to the front of the house. When she arrived there was no one there. Stepping out onto the porch she peered into the woods ahead of her. Seeing nothing she returned to the house and Abigail. Still it was something about the air. Turning just before she closed the door she was sure she had seen movement in the trees. She would mention it to John when he returned this evening.

Pushing it from her mind she returned to the candle making until it was time to prepare the evening meal. Glancing over at her sister, Mary noticed how Abigail was looking tired lately. They had been so excited when found out she was to have a child that she wondered if Abigail had been neglecting herself. It would be the first baby in the family for some time. Oh, there were distant cousins somewhere. Nothing near them. Mary couldn't even remember if she had met them as a child. With Mary and Abigail being the only children on this side each new day became an exciting new adventure. It was twofold as their husbands John and Will were the last descendants of their line. So for the four it was a brand new beginning. Even the most simple as shopping for baby shirts became a major wonder.

The women had gone to the mainland the week before to shop for the baby and Abigail had seen a small silver box in the window of one of the stores. She had looked at it with such longing that Mary knew she had to buy it for her. She watched her sister smile as Abigail ran her fingers lovingly over the little rosebuds on the lid. Then her expression changed as she slipped it back on the shelf and moved across the store to the more sensible purchases. It took only a moment for Mary to decide. She made the purchase and slipped it into her bag before Abigail turned her way. She smiled at her sister, happy to know that besides the baby this would be one of her most prized possessions. A warm feeling flowed over knowing this would be a new start for the Bale family.

Coming out of her reverie she realized it was time to put the candles away for another day. She paused a moment longer to smile at her younger sister cleaning up their work area. Then she turned and made her way to the kitchen to prepare the evening meal.

CHAPTER 14

Tom had been busy since daybreak setting up for the night's festivities. He was more than a little annoyed as his committee had been a no show. Andy was away on the mainland picking up supplies so he was off the hook so to speak. However, Emily had been missing all day. She hadn't shown up for work this morning at the café and no one had seen her since the day before, when she had worked a short shift before meeting Sheila. It would be just like her and Andy to slip over to the mainland to catch a few hours together before the night blew up around them.

On checking this morning he found that there were at least 100 visitors from the mainland over for the All Hallows Eve celebration. He had spoken to Sheila this morning and she promised to be there to help him as soon as she made a hurried visit to her grandfather. She had been feeling a bit guilty at not seeing him before now. If she stood outside the schoolhouse she could see the roof of her grandfathers' house and being this close there was a lot of guilt. The year that Sheila had lived there the four friends had spent most of their time at the stables at her grandfathers' house.

It had been a summer of fairy tales and fantasies. Tom and Andy had been close friends since the first grade and Sheila and Emily had been friends nearly as long. So when Sheila and her mother came to spend a year with her grandfather it sealed their friendship. Now on this day a memory long forgotten slipped back into his mind. No that wasn't quite true. It was more like there was no memory of it at all.

He vaguely remembered Sheila, Emily, Andy and himself meeting after dark at the stables. After bobbing for apples and the toasting of marshmallows they had been told they were too young for the rest of the evening and had been sent home to bed. This had not set well for four 10 year olds and they decided as soon as it was safe they would hide in the stables to watch. That was where his memory ended.

Picking up wood from the pile at his feet he proceeded to lay it outside the school for the night's bonfire. It looked like he was going to be doing everything on his own as his three friends had not turned up as they said they would. Piling more wood in his arms he made his way across the yard to the spot where the fire would be set. He wondered why all of a sudden the island people had decided to celebrate the night. It had been 10 years since the last one. Ten years. He was 10 years old the last time. Was this a significant number he wondered?

He stood for a moment gazing off into the woods. It had always seemed a scary place to him as a boy and he knew he would never have entered it if it hadn't been for his friends. However, he wasn't about to let them know he was afraid. It was because of this that he had agreed to slip back after dark to watch what the adults were doing. They had climbed up into the hayloft of Sheila's grandfather's barn and watched as the adults with lit torches wove their way through the woods toward them and this is where the memory stopped. He wondered if the others remembered more about that night. He would have to ask them if they finally turned up.

Realizing he had enough wood he turned toward the schoolhouse to see if there was anything else needed in the area. All looked complete. Satisfied he went into the school house to set up the tables and chairs for the evening meal. Looking around he saw the men who had been there earlier had pretty much finished everything. A podium stood at the front of the hall pushed back until it was needed for the Professor who was considered the main event of the evening. Now this was one person he did remember.

Even though the children had not been allowed to stay to hear him speak he remembered they were all frightened at his appearance. He had entered the schoolhouse while the children were still there. He was dressed in long black robes and had a very sinister appearance. Tom smiled at the thought that even after all these years seeing the professor again would put the childhood fears back in his heart. He felt for the children who would see him tonight.

The opening of the front door shook his reverie and turning around to the sound he saw Emily and Andy hand in hand slipping in. He set down the papers he was holding and made his way toward them. After they touched base each went their own way to finish up the few things left. Tom read over his own notes making a check point at each item to be sure everything was finished. During the professors speech he had arranged for several of the men to meet Sheila at her cottage for the candles to set up the trail for the candle walk. Then Emily and Andy would go over the chant with the crowd. There really wasn't too much to it.

The crowd would then start off lighting their candles by the stationery ones the men had set up and through a trail of lighted candles and flashing lights make their way from the schoolhouse to the cottage where the candles would go out and the witches and ghosts would appear on terror trail. Then they would follow to the mansion where the final coffee and sweets would be served. It would probably be midnight by the time everything was finished but all would feel they had their moneys' worth and would return to their homes feeling well entertained.

What he didn't know or have on his list was that Emily and Andy had spent the entire afternoon setting up a sound system to accompany the ghosts and witches set up by the men earlier. This was to be the final surprise for all, even their two friends. Sheila had slipped away to her cottage to pick up the candles for the trail and Emily was busy helping the women pack up the leftovers to be used tomorrow for whatever else had been planned.

Tom decided to join Andy at the back of the room to listen to the professor tell the tale of Wreath Island as they had been turned away from this as children. Everyone grew quiet as the professor stepped to the podium and looked out at the sea of faces before him. Then he turned on the reading light and began his tale.

Suddenly fear struck the professor and an all too familiar scene flashed before his eyes. It was at this moment that he knew he should not have come back. He also knew that the memories he would have tonight would not be good ones. Then he saw them standing in the dimness of the lights, Chief Jackson and the Reverend Carter. Ropes trailing from their hands that were tied around the necks of two men and two women.

The beating wings of four crows were heard and the sound of a small baby crying. It was as if the crying sound came from the crows as they flew over the crowd and called out their mournful cry. A heavy wind lifted the grass and swirled around the swinging feet of the four hanging there until they faded out of sight. It was over. Then with shaking hands he clutched the side of the podium and he remembered.

CHAPTER 15

Sheila stepped inside the door of her grandfathers' house. As a child she had always been in awe of the beauty of this place. She realized she hadn't thought too much about the house before now as the school and her own little cottage had taken priority over everything else. Now she stood looking around her at the grandeur of her grandfathers' home. She remembered very little about the year she had lived here. She remembered the stables most of all as this was where she and her three friends had spent most of their summer that year.

It was strange but the thing she remembered the most was the schoolhouse and the last night there in the stable. After that night her mother had packed them up and returned to the mainland. Until now she had forgotten the excitement of the last night. The games the children had played and the food and then the children had been sent home to bed so the adults could play their games. Something happened that night that she couldn't quite remember. Everything after they had crawled up into the hayloft in the stable became foggy in her mind and the harder she tried to remember the further the memory faded into the past.

She realized she had been standing just inside the doorway and reached back to close the door. She was then aware of the silence. It was as if no one ever lived here. She knew this wasn't true as Tom had told her that her grandfather did not leave the house any longer. It looked as though it was up to her to seek him out. Starting to check the first floor she followed the hall toward the kitchen area. This had been her domain while she stayed in the house. It always seemed so warm and friendly, not at all like the rest of the house so cold and formal.

She didn't really know her grandfather very well as he had no time for small children and she was sure he probably thought of her in the same way today. She had thought he would interfere with her taking the position at the school but there had been nothing from him on the matter. Sheila expected on their meeting today that it might come up so she was prepared. Moving across the large kitchen she ran her finger along the scrubbed table top. Everything had always been hard for Sheila. She found herself quite alone on the death of her father and mother. Suddenly there was a sharp flash of memory as she touched the table. There appeared in the centre a bonfire piled high with wood blazing in the dark followed by a mist and the sound of a child's voice and the pounding of horses hooves. As fast as it appeared it was gone.

Sheila stepped back from the table breathless from her insight. It seemed very familiar yet she could not hold it. She knew she would have to pursue it further but for now she had to find her grandfather and then join Tom to help with preparing for the night ahead. With a final glance around the room she continued back up the hall to grandfathers' study. Tentatively she opened the heavy wooden door into the inner sanctum of her grandfathers' life.

The room was dark and smoky and smelled of very old books. Although the windows had no covering the room seemed very dark for the time of day. She walked to the window and looked out over the forest to the spot where the schoolhouse stood. Surprisingly from this angle of the house the school could be seen quite clear. Even with the seeming overcast the little building was recognizable. She would have to look at the house from the school to see if it could be seen as clearly. Glancing around she noticed that the fireplace had been disturbed. It was as if someone had swept a hand over the surface clearing everything onto the floor.

Moving closer she found small pieces of what appeared to be glass over the mantle. The hearth held the appearance of a fresh fire and the remains of something having been burnt recently. Kneeling down she reached in and took a piece of burnt paper from the remains. Most of the message had been burnt away except for a small corner. She could barely read what it said for the dark burns around it. Sheila was only able to make out two words. 'The End'. The end, the end of what she wondered. She had been concentrating so hard on the words that she failed to notice the smoke rising from the fireplace and surrounding her. Looking up she saw the face of a small child looking back at her from the embers. She couldn't move and sat there clutching the piece of paper watching as a hand moved toward her.

Everything was very quiet and as she watched the smoke became more intense and the child's face became clearer to her. Then just as the hand was about to touch her face she fell back onto the floor and the smoke faded away taking the child with it. For a moment she lay on the floor wondering what had just happened. Looking up at the mantle she saw that it had also been disturbed and the little box that had been there for as long as she remembered was missing. Pulling herself up she ran her hand behind the things still standing on the mantle. No it was gone. She had admired it as a child but grandfather had never let her touch it nor would he touch it himself to show it to her. Now it was gone.

She would have to tell Andy, if her grandfather did not return home that the box had been stolen. Just as she was about to turn away she noticed something shining in the ashes on the hearth. Reaching down she pulled a silver chain from under the coals. Bringing it up into the light she realized it was a silver locket now tarnished from the fire that had nearly consumed it.

She went to the window and holding it up to the light she opened the clasp. As it fell open in her hand she saw the picture of a small child on the knee of an elderly man. The picture had been taken in front of the fireplace and the child was holding a small silver box in her hands. Moving closer into the light Sheila held the locket up where she could see the faces of the two people. She nearly dropped the locket in surprise for the two people in the locket were herself and her grandfather. Around her neck was the silver locket she now held. Clasped in her hand was the small silver box that grandfather had never let her touch. Grasping the locket tightly she rushed from the room. She wasn't sure what had just happened but deep down she knew she had just found the first piece of a long lost puzzle.

The house seemed even more frightening now she had fit some of the puzzles pieces together. She held the box and locket close to her. Even in fear she knew that they were important in her life and she would have to keep them near her at all times. She also knew she would have to ask grandfather the meaning of both, regardless of how frightening the outcome would be. She had to get out and back to her own cottage and fast. She knew her life could be in great danger. She rushed to the door and flew from the room never looking back.

CHAPTER 16

Sheila raced out of the front door of her grandfathers' house. She was sure she missed every step in her haste to get away. She had to get back to her cottage without someone seeing her. She wasn't sure what she had just seen but something about it frightened her so badly she had to leave. Her hands shook as she tried to open her front door and after dropping her keys twice did manage to fall into the room.

Closing the door behind her Sheila slipped to the floor her whole body shaking. Why was she so frightened? Was it the picture of her with her grandfather, or not being able to remember having one taken with him? She should have remembered for she was not a small child in the picture but more the age of ten when she stayed there for a full year. She reached in her pocket and touched the box that the grandfather had forbidden her to touch or even come near all the time she had lived in his mansion. Reaching into her pocket once again she pulled out the snapshot. Even touching it made her recoil.

Looking down she realized the silver box was now sitting on her lap. She thought back to the mantle earlier today and knew she hadn't seen the box there then. Yet here it was in her lap. It had always been tucked behind the heavy candle holders as long as she could remember. She had looked for it today. She had moved everything aside and had found nothing. Not even a dust mark to show where it had rested; now it was here in her hand. She fingered the snapshot once more and still having the same sensation slipped it back into her pocket. There was something not right here.

Suddenly the room began to darken and Sheila moved further away from the door. There was a sudden noise sounding like a hundred birds wings flapping around the room causing Sheila to crouch further into a nearby corner. She could feel the breeze as the birds flew around her head and the air became very heavy. She had never known such fear. She crawled further into the corner and crouched there, fearful they might follow her. It was like a blanket of black until just above her vision she saw them taking shape. They were headed toward her, a large flock of black crows, wings flapping wildly. She covered her eyes and curled into a tight ball just as they came overhead. Then they were gone.

Everything became very quiet, dropping stillness over the entire room. Sheila lay very still for just a moment. When nothing happened, she slowly lifted her head and to her surprise there was nothing there, the crows were gone. She was quite alone. What had just happened? Slowly she moved her head from side to side. To her surprise there was no evidence of what she had just seen.

She had never been comfortable when she had stayed at her grandfathers' house even with her mother there to keep her safe. Funny she should think of having protection now that she was back. Now sitting here on her floor she felt suddenly more afraid than she had ever been as a child. She longed for her mother and the safety she brought.

Taking a deep breath she pushed her way to a standing position. Still leaning against the door she felt a sudden change in the air. The air was fresher and the darkness had faded away. It took a moment for her to compose herself. Then doing the few things she had to do around the house she made herself ready for the evening. One more glance to see if there was anything out of place and finally she slipped her key in the cottage door and headed back toward the schoolhouse.

Heading up the laneway she had the odd feeling that someone was behind her. She turned and looking back toward the house stopped dead in her tracks. The whole house seemed to be enveloped in fog. Looking upwards to the roof of the house she felt a sudden chill watching as the fog took the form of a great winged horse and perched atop it was the figure of a tiny child. Their eyes locked for just a moment then the vision disappeared. Slipping her hand into her pocket she reached once more for the photograph. Just as her fingers touched it the chill returned and the photo was gone. Turning she fled the final steps to the school house.

CHAPTER 17

Professor Fuller stood at the back of the ferry watching the mainland fade from view. Not for the first time did he wonder if this could be a mistake. The last time he had been the guest speaker on this occasion it had ended with the disappearance of the local school teacher. He was sure that hearing the story of the islands history had just frightened her into breaking her contract and fleeing the island. Since then there had been no communication from her and no one really knew what had happened. Had there been foul play he was sure that the island constable would have notified the mainland and the news would have been published in the local newspaper.

He had called the local newspaper office twice but there had been no news of any disappearance on that night or any other night for that matter. He finally had to accept the fact and set the night aside which he did. Now it was all returning and he couldn't help but feel that he was in some way responsible for it all. Stepping back from the rail he made his way to the front of the boat for his first view of the island. There was a haze over the water tonight giving the island a somewhat eerie look. He didn't remember if the last time there was a full moon or not or if there had been a haze. Had there been he might have felt the cold air that now surrounded him and he would have returned to the mainland.

He turned toward the cabin where the captain was starting to gear down the boat for docking. The fog seemed deeper here and he was unable to see anyone at the helm. He walked toward the door that enclosed the cabin to ask the captain how long he would be docked before heading back to the mainland. Just as he was about to open the door the boat lurched against the dock sending him up against the row of chairs standing against the wall. It took a minute or so to right himself and when he did he realized the captain was heading up the gangplank to the island dock. Brushing off his clothes he stepped down from the boat and followed the captain up the hill.

He would have to find Tom and let him know that he was not going to be unable to speak. He would have to do some thinking since he was already on the island. However, he was sure he would come up with some reason. Looking ahead he realized the captain had disappeared from his view. There was no way he could have passed him nor could the captain have returned to the boat without him knowing. Once again there was a feeling of foreboding. There was such a chill in the air he felt the need to pull his collar up tight around his neck.

Turning he looked back toward the place the boat had docked. He also noticed in this short time the fog had lifted. The sky was perfectly clear now with no fog or haze visible. Not only were they gone but the boat was gone also. He was left on the island with no way of returning this night. Panic overcame him for this was the last boat back to the mainland until the next day. With sudden fear he pulled his coat tight around his shoulders and started once more up the hill. It was too late to go back now. He couldn't help but think he was repeating a night from 10 years ago.

Since there was nothing else to do but go on he made his way up the hill to the little school house in the woods. This was where everything would begin. He understood that this year there was a new school teacher. He wondered if he should use the word begin. The word might be alright. However, it was the word 'end' he feared as the last time it did not work well. He paused for just a moment at the path leading to the school wondering why he had said yes to the letter, then shoulders back headed toward the night.

CHAPTER 18

Tom looked around the grounds in front of the school house. It looked like everything was ready. Sheila had finally arrived and between them they had made things ready for the night. Emily and Andy still hadn't turned up to help and Tom made a mental note to give them what for when they did return. Not that he blamed them for he would also welcome a trip to the mainland once in a while. Living on the island had some benefits but it was lonely at times.

Looking over toward the tree lined path he noticed Sheila standing looking off into the distance. He remembered her as a child day dreaming most of the time looking off into the trees for her fairies and unicorns. Her world seemed almost separate from the other three. Still they had been good friends as children and he welcomed the chance to renew that friendship now. He was just about to walk over her way when a group of local ladies arrived loaded down with food for the evening. By the time he had shown them around Sheila had moved over to another group involved in a lengthy conversation.

Turning back towards the fire pit he checked once more to see if there was enough wood and if the barricade was sufficient to keep the children from falling into the fire. He also checked to see if the tubs were filled with water for bobbing with apples and tightened the strings along the porch that would hold apples for another fun game. He could hear laughter as groups made their way up the hill eager for the night to start. The sun was just starting to set and Tom could see the fog coming in over the bay. He looked back through the trees and watched as the shadows began to fall as they did every evening at this time of the year.

At this point everything seemed to be normal making the evening seem like a probable success. So far even the children seemed to be enjoying themselves which looked after one problem. Entertaining them until the food was served. He decided to join Sheila to see if she had noticed anything amiss and check on Emily and Andy to make sure they had covered all the loose ends.

He was almost to her when a hand reached out and touched his shoulder. He swung back ready to defend himself. He was surprised to see Professor Fuller standing in front of him a look of fear on his face. Sheepishly he reached toward the retreating professor. It took a moment or two to explain to him that he had his mind on something else and that the man had just startled him. Taking the professors' arm he steered him toward the campfire and a group of chatting people. One of the men brought him a cold drink and perched him on a log to watch the antics of the children.

Tom glanced toward the cottage in the woods. He could see the mist starting to form over the roof. As he watched, not for the first time, it seemed to form the shape of a winged horse carrying a small child. He could hear the sound of wings as it rose into the sky. He shook himself realizing he must be daydreaming. Looking towards the spot where Sheila had been standing he noticed that she too was looking over the cottage. The look on her face matching the one on his, a look of memory. Then it came, the tinkling sound of a child's voice as four figures ropes dangling around their necks rose from the cottage one at a time and swept over the trees. As they reached the treetops Sheila moved toward the path that led to the cottage and her home.

Just as she reached the start of the small pathway that would lead to her door she paused and looked back. Tom was standing at the bonfire watching her. She managed a small wave then turning continued on. She wished that Emily was with her however, she didn't want her friends to think that she was afraid. Yet she was afraid and couldn't put her finger on why. It had been 10 years since she had walked these paths but tonight it seemed like yesterday. She could just see the roof of the cottage ahead. Quickening her step she hurried to the small porch and taking her key from her pocket slipped it in the lock.

Reaching inside the door she flicked the light switch and realizing there was no light she crossed to the kitchen area to find candles. She had found them there the first night when she arrived. They were beautifully hand crafted in a luminous black. They must have been crafted for resale as she had found a further carton in the bedroom closet. Possibly the school teacher that had lived here when she was a child had made them as a pastime when she wasn't teaching with the thought of selling them at the island craft shows. Whatever the reason they would come in handy for her now and also to light the pathway on the first lap of the evenings' entertainment.

Taking the box with her, she wandered the room setting each one in the holders already in place. By the time she finished she had 13 pillars of black gleaming throughout the room. Now with all the light she noticed the silver box on her desk. Crossing she picked it up and sitting crossed legged on the floor placed it in her lap. Running her fingers softly over the top she moved along the front of the box until she found the clasp. Moving it upwards she opened the lid.

It was then the box began to glow. At first just a glimmer but as she put pressure on the clasp the box began to glow until it outshone the 13 candles in the room. Sheila tried to move her hand but something in the box held her and she was powerless to break the link. As she watched the 13 candles became brighter until the night around her was no longer dark but glowed like the morning sun.

It was then Sheila knew fear as she never had before. She felt the box move in her hand and from it trailed a long silver chain which wound slowly around her wrist. It tightened for just a moment then with one final glow dropped a silver oval in her hand. Slowly lowering her eyes she found she was holding the locket from her grandfather's house. The air had once again become heavy and she was unable to breath. A voice came to her saying "now that you have the locket you're branded a witch. It is the duty of the witch hunter to end your life". Sheila began to tremble, for now she understood the fear she had always felt for her grandfather.

As she watched, the locket opened revealing the picture of her grandfather and herself holding the silver box. The chain circled around her wrist and wound itself tightly until she could no longer free herself. Fear began to overtake her and she felt herself beginning to drift into blackness. Her final moment of consciousness was of 13 candles one by one flickering into extinction.

CHAPTER 19

Tom glanced up at the sky. It seemed to be almost sunset. Glancing at his watch he realized it was a bit early for the festivities to start. They would have to speed things up in order to have the children fed and sent back to their homes before dark. It had been decided that they should not be present for the professor's talk or during the walk as it might frighten them. Wreath Island had always been a bit of a mystery. There had been rumours of hangings on the island during the time of the witch trials in the 1800's and even since that time. It had been said and still was for that matter that when the moon was full you could still hear the screams coming from the front yard of the small cottage kept for the local school teacher.

This cottage had not been used since the last school teacher had left them 10 years before. She had disappeared the night of All Hallows Eve and never been heard from since. If this was to be part of the professor's speech it would be enough to keep half the village children awake all night. Investigation at the time turned up nothing. The sheriff had tried notifying her family but after several months with no leads filed it as an unsolved case and went on to other things. Just like that he thought her life was over and discarded.

On entering the school house he found that Emily and Andy had everything well under control. Most of the families were already enjoying the food set out by the local women's group and you could hear the chatter and tinkle of dishes in the makeshift kitchen at the other end of the hall. Some of the children had already been herded off home to give their parents a few hours of entertainment without them.

The men with Emily in charge were stacking tables and beginning to set up chairs for the professors segment of the evening. When finally the last child had been sent down to their various beds a stage was set up with podium and reading light for the professor. At last all was ready for All Hallows Eve. Tom reached his hand toward the light switch on the wall and flicking it twice announced that Professor Fuller was about to begin. As everything became quiet Tom took a seat at the back and settled down to finally hear the story he had missed 10 years earlier. The history of Wreath Island.

Everyone was quiet as the professor stepped up to the podium. Turning on the reading light he gazed out into the audience. Suddenly fear struck him and an all too familiar scene flashed before his eyes. It was at this moment he knew that he should not have come. He also knew that the memories that would come back to him tonight would not be good ones. For their standing before him in the dim light stood the sheriff and the parson, ropes trailing from their hands that were tied around the necks of two men and two women. They stood in silence as overhead the sound of flapping wings were heard and with them the tinkling of a small child's voice. Then he remembered.

Tom's time out to hear the professor was short lived. The professor had just started his introduction when one of the men tapped Tom on the shoulder and motioned him outside. The men he had sent on to the cottage to pick up the candles from Sheila had returned saying the cottage was dark and there had been no answer when they knocked on the door. After several loud knocks they had returned to the school house to see if Sheila had misunderstood and returned there with the candles.

When they couldn't find her they sought out Tom to see if she was in fact in trouble.

CHAPTER 20

Tom had some misgivings as he and several of the men made their way to the cottage to see if there was a problem. They had only gone a short distance when they could see a slight flicker of light ahead of them. It could only come from the cottage as there was nothing else between them and the school house. The men assured him there had been no light when they were there the first time.

Making their way up the steps they tapped lightly on the door. It was opened immediately by a surprised Sheila. When asked why the lights had been out she assured them the cottage lights had been on since she arrived and that there had been no knock on the door as she would have heard it. After a slight discussion she crossed the room and taking four cartons of candles from the counter she gave them to the men who then left to place them along the path into the woods in preparation for the walk. The walk was the only area to have candles and each person would be given one to carry as well.

Terror Trail would follow with its own version of terror. The finale would be at the mansion with a massive show of fireworks then after food and drink would send people home to bed happy with the evening they had shared. It wasn't a complicated program as no one seemed to have a lot of inspiration when it was set up. However, with the professor there to start things it appeared to be entertaining enough.

Deciding it was too late to go back to catch the professors' talk he would go on with the men and help make up the time they had lost in setting up the first lap. Sheila would go back to help Emily and Andy start the people with their chant and start them on their way. All in all it had the makings of a great final weekend of the season. Closing the cottage door he handed the key to Sheila. He stood for a moment on the tiny stoop and gazed into the tall trees just behind the cottage. At night they had a sinister look about them and Tom wished the evening would end right here at the cottage door rather than take a herd of people off into something that looked this way. Laughing at his own thoughts he waved at Sheila and made his way down the steps to follow the men into the woods.

Sheila turned and waved to Tom and the men who set off to put the candles in the holders they had set along the trail. From the entrance to the woods they had set up witches and ghosts in the trees and Tom had set speakers to set the right atmosphere. She smiled as she thought of the people making their way, candles in hand waiting to be startled. Everyone wanted to believe in the afterlife as being made up of ghosts that hung around just to frighten the people left. Yet witches more than anything seemed to be able to keep people in their homes after dark on the chance that one might be lurking around the next corner.

Sheila wasn't afraid of ghosts nor was she afraid of witches. The ghosts always seemed such a silly thing to her. They were just something that came out on Halloween to add to the night. They were never more than candy that was handed out at every door. The witches now that was another thing. It seemed people were more afraid of them. Otherwise why did they put people on trial and then put them to death if witches were not real. She had always been fascinated by the trials of the 1800's. There had been so many women put to death because their neighbours and friends had labelled them witches. So much fear and why?

There had been rumours that right here on the island a family of witches had been hung. She had tried to find records of this but there had been none available either on the island or the mainland. Deciding it had been just another old wives tale she finally gave up. She wished she had been able to hear the professor speak tonight as he may have given some inkling as to the truth of the story. Glancing to her right she was aware of a small light that seemed to be moving as she moved. She watched as it shifted to the area where the men were still setting up the candles. It seemed to be following them up the path. As they stopped, it stopped then went on as they did.

Quickly turning off to the right she made her way to the area where the men were working. The light could still be seen moving down the path over the heads of the men who seemed oblivious of anything happening. She didn't feel fear for herself but for some reason felt the men might be in danger. Running she caught up with them all the time watching the light overhead. It was then she knew this meant danger. The fear she felt earlier was more intense this time and she wished her friends were with her now. For some reason the dark was more intense and the air less like haze and more solid to push through.

Just as she reached the men the light went out leaving only the light from the candles on the path. Searching the trees she found nothing. Then just as she decided it had been her imagination because of the night, she heard it. The tiny sound of laughter she had heard before. A slight breeze wafted through the trees and with it a vision she had tried to suppress. Then all returned to normal and she stood alone with the witches and ghosts flying overhead.

CHAPTER 21

Emily and Andy finished up the tables in the school house. Everything else had been cleaned up by the ladies in charge of the food. They had worked during the professors' speech so they could join the group on their trek through the woods. No one wanted to miss out on the entertainment that would complete the summer for the residents and visitors on the island. There had been quite a crowd as the island had offered a night of fun, food and fright.

At first they were just going to put up a few lights, then set off for an afternoon across the Bay. However, the more they thought about it the more excited they were about the night to come. The Bay would always be there but what they were doing this afternoon in the woods could be a onetime thing. They decided they would give people their fun and fright. The food would just be a plus.

Emily smiled as she thought of the sound system she and Andy had set up in the woods. They had let Tom and Sheila think they had gone off to the mainland for an afternoon's fun and then had spent it instead stringing wires through the trees along the path. It was set so the moment the crowd entered the area they would be accosted by witches and ghosts flying overhead. Andy had contributed the sound of moaning and the cackling of witches to finish the picture.

They had also placed fans so a breeze would blow out their candles just as the sound came on leaving them in the dark with ghosts and witches flying overhead. They had such fun putting this together and wanted to be there when it happened. There had been no thought that this might frighten some of the crowd just a little too much. Now with the tables stacked and the chairs put away they were finally ready to check out their handy work. The candle walk had just started as they arrived so they cut across a path leading behind the cottage to a short cut into the woods. Everything was very dark except for the candles carried by the crowd. It was set up so the first person crossing the line to the next area would trigger the beginning.

A line had been set up ankle height at the last candle. It had been concealed so there was no way it could be missed by the first foot stepping forward. They could hear chants and see the flickering lights as the group moved along the path making their way into the woods. Staying well back in the trees they smiled as they waited for the show to begin. Suddenly in the sky just above them there appeared a tiny light. It was no larger than you might see looking up at the stars at night. It seemed to be moving toward them. Neither of them spoke as they watched it move downwards from the trees settling almost in front of them. Neither could move transfixed as they were.

It slowly moved backward and forward in front of them to a point where had they been able to move they could have reached out and touched it. Then as one, a suppressed memory formed in their minds, something from the past. Then it was gone and all they were left with was the tinkling sound of a child's laughter and the darkness of the night.

CHAPTER 22

Chief Jackson finished the messages that had come in for him that day. He had left for the mainland with Reverend Carter early that morning to speak at the local Children's Association meeting. He had also arranged for his deputy Andy to take over the office while he was gone so had been in no hurry to get back to the island. Reverend Carter had also made himself available for the entire day so the chief looked forward to a day with his friend.

It had been an early meeting with the usual coffee and sweets provided to take the edge off any part of the speeches that might have a slight boring hint to them. Then a grand luncheon leaving the rest of the day free to them to see the sights. They were very close to Boston and he hoped that there would be enough time to go into the city and look around. However, by the time they had finished with the schedule set up for them they had just enough time to head back to the boat and home. He turned out the lights, then checking all the doors turned the key in the front door and headed for the church to pick up the minister.

Reverend Carter had just finished with his days messages and opened his mail when he saw the chief pulling up in front of the church. He sighed and wished he were not involved in any of the activities but for some reason the village committee felt that he and the chief should be up front in the All Hallows

Eve celebration. They should be just about on time for the meal at the school house and the history brought to them by Professor Fuller.

As he understood it the police chief and himself would start the walk and lead the group along Terror Trail to finish at the Old Man's mansion where once again there would be more food. If he thought about it the food part had been the most enjoyable part of the day. He worried a bit about some of the other things planned. Even the names had an eerie sound. Remembering how large the crowd seemed coming off the boat he wondered if raising terror in a crowd this size was a very good idea. Although fun was fun, some people tended to take too many things serious and not for the first time worried about the outcome.

Shuffling his papers together for the Sunday sermon once again he wondered if his inspiration would be enough to wash out the fear they were instilling this night. He was preparing for another All Hallows Eve. His thoughts wandered back to the first All Hallows Eve. Just a bit of fun it had been labelled. Yet before the night was over fear had been instilled in the village and the local school teacher had disappeared. Now 10 years later the same feeling was in the air and he worried what might happen this time. Still there was nothing he could do. With a shrug of his shoulders he pushed away from his responsibilities and went out to meet his friend.

Sighing he turned off the light on his desk and turning back to make sure all was as it should be he closed the door and left the church. Then leaving the chief's car at the church they walked side by side up the hill toward the school house and the night's festivities once more.

CHAPTER 23

Sheila stood waiting for everyone to take their place in line. She had to make sure everyone was started on the trail and then she would be able to take her place with the others at the mansion. That was the problem with being on a committee you were always left to make sure everything was done. Because of this you so often missed out on things yourself. Next year she would be sure she was just one of the group having fun.

She watched as the crowd began to fidget wanting to get started. They were just waiting for Sheriff Jackson and Reverend Carter to arrive. She had noticed them earlier lingering over the dessert table and supposed they were having a preview of the sweets that were to follow the walk. Just as she was about to go and track them down they came down the steps of the school house and headed toward the crowd. She breathed a sigh of relief as some of the crowd were showing signs of leaving.

She placed both men at the head of the group and instructed them what to do. Then beginning the chant that they would use along the candle walk she started them along their way. With a glance sideways at each other and a final sigh Reverend Carter and Sheriff Jackson lit their candles from the one mounted on the pole next to them. Each person followed and once their candles were lit chanting with excitement made their way into the woods. Sheila watched as the last two disappeared up the trail. They could be heard even after they were out of sight.

Looking around Sheila was suddenly aware of how dark it had become and wished someone had stayed behind with her. She wondered why with all the candles they had set there was so little light. She didn't look forward to making her way into the forest in the dark. Turning her back to the trail she slipped behind the school house and down the path that she and her friends had travelled so many times as children. Walking along the path she was once more aware of the darkness. It was as though all the candles had been extinguished. Then deciding it wasn't important she continued along the path to the spot that would bring her into the moving crowd.

As she walked she suddenly felt that she was not alone. Everything around her seemed ominous. She wondered if they might have been too authentic on their decorations. She could see ghosts and witches swinging overhead and wondered how frightening they would be when lights were turned on them. She could hear a crowd of people plodding their way through the brush. There was still some chanting but it seemed to have lost its feeling. Then suddenly everything was quiet and there was no light except on the luminous figures flying overhead.

Fear struck Sheila as she realized this was not the way they had planned the evening. It was as though someone else had taken over the entertainment leaving them spectators as well. Movement ahead stopped her in her tracks. She stood very still wondering what would happen next, when she heard Emily and Andy calling out to her. Pushing the brush aside she rushed toward them, safe at last. The three huddled together wondering why their plans had been altered and by who.

Slipping through the trees they joined the crowd huddled together in a small clearing. In the quietness it was as if time was frozen. The few small moans from one or two of the women were the only signs that there was of life. Then life began again as a soft breeze worked its way up the path toward them. All turned toward the cottage where the breeze seemed to originate. As they watched, the sky began to light up above the cottage. No one moved, they were so transfixed by the light. Sheila made a mental note to compliment whoever had arranged the special lighting as it certainly added to the fright factor.

Then as she watched, the roof of the cottage seemed to lift and rising from it came four figures. Two men and two women, each holding a length of rope that was tied tightly around their necks. They circled the cottage once then slowly made their way toward the crowd. Sheila turned toward her friends to ask who had made it possible. Seeing the looks on their faces she knew that they knew no more than she did. She wondered if she would ever be able to enter the cottage again.

Then as fast as it had happened it was gone. Once more the path was lit and also the area around the crowd. The three friends slipped out of the trees and joined the group below. There was a quiet rumble of voices as everyone discussed what had just happened and what would happen next. Emily found herself moving closer to Andy as the crowd began to move once more. Just as they began to relax and move up the trail the fireworks started and the once dark area became as day. Andy chuckled a little thinking what a good job Tom had done in this area. The crowd gave its usual sound of appreciation just in time as it was in not more than five minutes that the darkness fell once again.

Then in the quiet a light appeared ahead of them on the path. To the right a spotlight flashed upon four large trees directly in their path. For a moment it was just the trees, then one by one a body appeared hanging and moving slowly in the breeze. A man and a woman, then a man and a woman who was with child. The last woman looking straight into the eyes of the parson and the sheriff. As she swung to and fro on the branch she raised her right arm and pointed first at the minister and then the sheriff. Then lifting her hand to the minister she slowly opened it and dropped into his hand a small glowing silver box. As it reached him a piercing scream surrounded the cowering crowd. A clap of thunder shook the ground and from overhead came the sound of large wings beating against the wind and the tinkle of laughter of a small child.

Tom sat on an overturned trough in front of the stables. At one time this had been an active happy place. People came from the mainland to see the wonderful horses kept here. Also a club used the stable for an equestrian group from the mainland. He remembered the time that Sheila had lived at the mansion and they were allowed to ride the horses under supervision. That seemed like such a long time ago. This had been when Sheila and her mother had lived with Sheila's grandfather after her father had passed away suddenly.

He remembered only small parts. Like the times in the woods where the magic happened. They were all 10 years old and still into fantasies of childhood. Many days they were privileged to see fairies and unicorns prancing in the sun. As the summer went on the fairies became less afraid of them so by the time All Hallows Eve arrived they had become fast friends and protectors. He suddenly realized he had been somewhere in the past. He hadn't done this for a very long time. There had always been a line that he couldn't cross when it came to his childhood. Memories, no matter how hard he tried, always seemed to fade away just as they came to the consciousness. Now for some reason the memories were flooding back faster than he could control them.

CHAPTER 24

Finding his hands shaking he fought to control them and the thoughts racing through his head. He knew that if he pursued this further something would come to him that he didn't want to know. In the distance he could hear the sound of the fireworks and the noise of the crowd making their way through the woods. They would be here soon and then the evening would be complete. For some reason he felt uncomfortable and wanted it over.

Overhead the sky was lighting up from the fireworks and the closer the crowd came the brighter it became. Tom stood and started towards the opening to the woods. He was able to see the crowd and noted it was being led by a tiny shining light acting almost like a beacon for them. It bobbed from side to side almost like an excited child who knows a treat is at the end of its journey. Tom stopped and waited to see what would happen next. Soon the light was upon him and the dark was closing in behind the crowd coming up the trail.

When they had reached him they stopped, the sheriff and the parson still in the lead all looking over his head. He watched as the expression on their faces changed from curiosity to fear. Turning slowly he followed their gaze to four large trees at the stable with a corpse swinging from a long frayed rope on each slowly as if in a breeze. Turning back to the crowd he also found them watching. He moved to the sheriff hoping he would have the answer to what was happening. He saw only the same fear on his face that registered on the crowd around him. Then he turned to a person who stood hand outwards holding a small silver box. The crowd remained silent as if watching a play unfold and not wanting to miss any of the drama.

Movement from the back brought his attention to three people pushing toward him. It was Sheila along with Emily and Andy. They were moving side to side to get nearer to him. A silence had fallen over the entire area. The only sound was that of the crackling fire that had been set for the final coffee hour to complete the night. It blazed much higher than it had earlier and Tom made a mental note that as soon as he talked to his three friends he would bank it to a more logical height.

As the three moved the rest of the crowd followed them until all were standing just under where the people were hanging. Tom made a move to go to the fire, but found it had begun to move closer putting everyone in danger. As the last person had been forced to position at the foot of the trees he made a last move toward the fire. Now he found that the fire was no longer contained but seemed to be following the crowd. The tiny light was ushering them into a tight circle at the foot of the trees and the fire followed suit. When all had been pushed as tight as possible the tiny light circled around their heads making sure they were all watching the trees. Then with tiny somersaults it bounced up to the last woman hanging there and nestled in her arms.

The silver box in the parsons' hand began to glow and rising slowly it flew to the top of the stable stopping long enough to light up the window at the top where four little faces peered down at the scene below. It paused for only a moment then dropped a glowing silver necklace into the hand of one of the little girls sitting there. Just as the necklace settled in her hand the flames from the fire escalated surrounding the stable and the scene before it. Great wings sounded overhead blanking out the sounds from the people as the flames washed over them. Tom along with Sheila and his friends stood together looking up at the stable door above them. There was no sound coming from the crowd as the flames engulfed them. The chief and the parson were as statues eyes glazed to the scene before them. Then as if from nowhere a large winged bird came from the smoke and erased the scene. All Hallows Eve had come to an end.

EPILOGUE/ASHES

Tom stood at the edge of what had been a popular summer spot for many Boston residents from July 4th weekend up to the popular All Hallows Eve celebration that had been held every year till that one fatal one. It had made the island the most visited summer area in Boston. Looking over the water now it was hard to remember how appealing it had been to so many people. The clear blue of the water seemed to entice anyone standing there to enter the small tourist boats available to all and make their journey small as it was out to sea. He remembered his childhood here and the adventures he had with his friends. Somewhere in his mind was a small corner he was unable to enter, no matter how hard he tried. He did remember his friends Sheila, Emily and Andy. At the thought of them he found his mind beginning to wander. A sudden rustle in the trees behind shook his reverie and what might have been a look into the past faded from his view.

Once more he gazed out over the water but this time became aware of the oily surface it held. It had every appearance of a winter skating rink and he could see himself with Sheila skimming across the glass surface. How happy things had been then. Once more his memory shifted for just a moment then faded from sight and he strained to keep it with him to no avail. Looking over the area he could see where his island had been. Now the boat docks were gone from both sides, washed away leaving no evidence of having been there. The trees on the shoreline, both sides were mere skeletons of what had been and the water held a murky appearance that led you to believe if you stepped out you could walk to the other side.

Tom wondered if this were true but was not eager to explore the thought. Somewhere overhead there was the sound of flapping wings and Tom peered through what trees were left to what the cause was. There was no sun peering between the branches making vision impossible. He moved closer to the water's edge and there just to his right was the figure of a gigantic bird coming toward him. It was showing every evidence of Tom being the reason it was there.

Soon it was close enough for him to make out the birds features and also to see there was a small something on its' back. The closer it came there was also a sound that could be a voice. He felt fear for the first time and he really did not want to know what it was. He huddled closer in the brush hoping it would pass over but soon realized this was not going to happen. The wings of the bird fanned the underbrush beside him and he pulled back trying to hide from whatever it was he might have to challenge. Now the voice became clear and he was able to distinguish it as that of a small child.

He was about to lift his head from hiding when a large wing swept over him and without touching the ground swept him up over the murky bay and into the sky. As the treetops settled down there was the sound of a small child's voice tinkling high above and the settling of ash once more over the ground until there was nothing but ash over the entire area and filtering down through it all came a tiny voice murmuring.

ASHES, ASHES, ASHES AND NOW IT'S OVER OR NOT

www.ingramcontent.com/pod-product-compliance
Lightning Source LLC
LaVergne TN
LVHW041536060526
838200LV00037B/1014